my spots

MW01089570

Created by Marina V.

Art by Victoria Usova

Copyright © 2016 Marina V.

All rights reserved.

ISBN-10: 1523685913
ISBN-13: 978-1523685912

Library of Congress Control Number: 2016901651
CreateSpace Independent Publishing Platform, North Charleston, SC

THIS BOOK BELONGS TO

_____

DEDICATION

I dedicate this book to my daughter Emilie Leonie Umali who inspired me to write it.

In memory of our Kisa, whose tiger stripes and leopard spots will always be remembered.

You're not the only one with spots.
Look at the spots nature created
on these animals.

Just like a

TIGER

has its stripes,

so do you.

Just like a

LEOPARD

has its spots,

so do you.

Just like a

BUTTERFLY

has beautiful lines,

Just like an

Appaloosa

has its dots,

so do you.

Some

are born

with spots and

some are not.

Baby

have spots that disappear

and then they look

like mama deer.

Just like a

FISH

has its marks,

Just like a

LADYBUG

has its spots

to count for luck,

Just like your birthmark,

it's there to mark a special you.

Whether on land like a

GIRAFFE

or like a fish in water,

or like a butterfly flying in the sky,

Nature creates birthmarks.

Be proud of your spots.

They're unique to you!

Where are your special *spots*?

Draw your birthmarks!

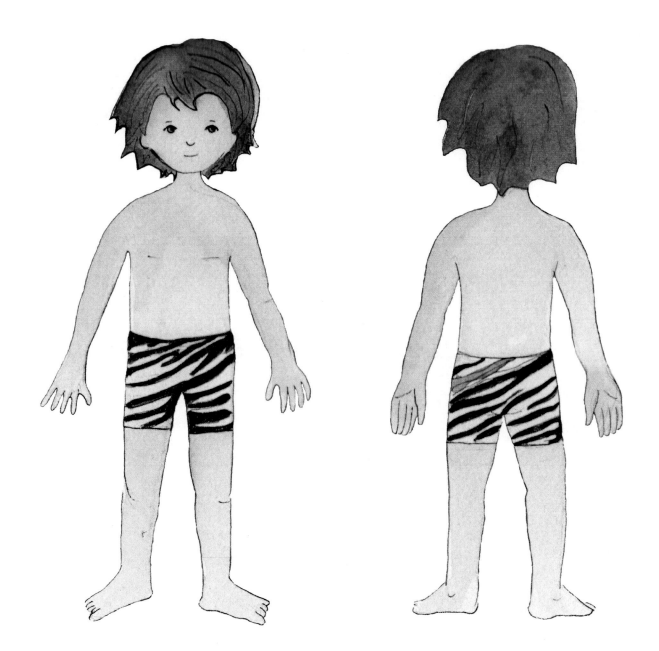

If you were an animal, what type

of *spots* would you have?

Draw here!

Thank you for reading my book.
If you enjoyed my book, I would love a review and lots of stars.

Feel free to connect with me on the web at
https://www.facebook.com/AuthorMarinaV or
write to me at marina@marinavdesignstudio.com

I look forward to hearing from you.

Marina

Made in United States
North Haven, CT
05 May 2023

36269776R00022